IN DIVISIBLE CITIES

In Divisible Cities

A Phanto-Cartographical Missive

Dominic Pettman

`dead letter office`

BABEL Working Group

punctum books ∗ brooklyn, ny

IN DIVISIBLE CITIES: A PHANTO-CARTOGRAPHICAL MISSIVE
© Dominic Pettman, 2013.

First published in 2013 by
dead letter office, BABEL Working Group
an imprint of punctum books
Brooklyn, New York
http://punctumbooks.com

The BABEL Working Group is a collective and desiring-assemblage of scholar-gypsies with no leaders or followers, no top and no bottom, and only a middle. BABEL roams and stalks the ruins of the post-historical university as a multiplicity, a pack, looking for other roaming packs and multiplicities with which to cohabit and build temporary shelters for intellectual vagabonds. We also take in strays.

ISBN-13: 978-0615853192
ISBN-10: 0615853196

Cover design and interior illustrations by Merritt Symes. Cover artwork: "Reflections on Sagrada Familia," by Ingrid Siliakus.

Editorial Team: Tim Harvey, Eileen Joy & Matt Schneider

indivisiblecities.com: website design by Alli Crandell

Visit INDIVISIBLECITIES.COM

Amsterdam

Barcelona

Canberra

Chicago

Geneva

Hong Kong

London

Melbourne

Napoli

New York

Paris

Philadelphia

Rome

Sydney

Taipei

Tokyo

Istanbul

Urville

Venice

ACKNOWLEDGMENTS

This book grew slowly over several years. What began as a series of mental postcards, with different addressees, eventually became a kind of city in itself, requiring more than one architect to make it work. I am therefore extremely grateful to the following people who helped turn this project into something you can now hold, read, click, zoom, and/or download. Alexandra Chasin gave me very helpful feedback on an early draft, helping to create a more coherent through-line. Yew Leong Lee breathed new life into the project by publishing an extract in *Asymptote*, also translated into Italian. Matt Schneider and Tim Harvey did a sterling job with editorial assistance. Merritt Symes fashioned the intriguing illustrations, re-rendering found images into something much more suggestive and enigmatic. Ingrid Siliakus was generous enough to let me use her stunning artwork for an ideal cover image. Alli Crandell spent an incredible amount of time and talent on developing the beautiful and mesmerizing virtual version of the book, which can be found at indivisiblecities.com. And thanks especially to Eileen Joy, for providing such an ideal home for a text about being essentially unhomed: the Dead Letter Office of punctum books. It is indeed a joy, and relief—like finally setting down one's heavy and battered suitcases—to find this particular journey at a welcoming end.

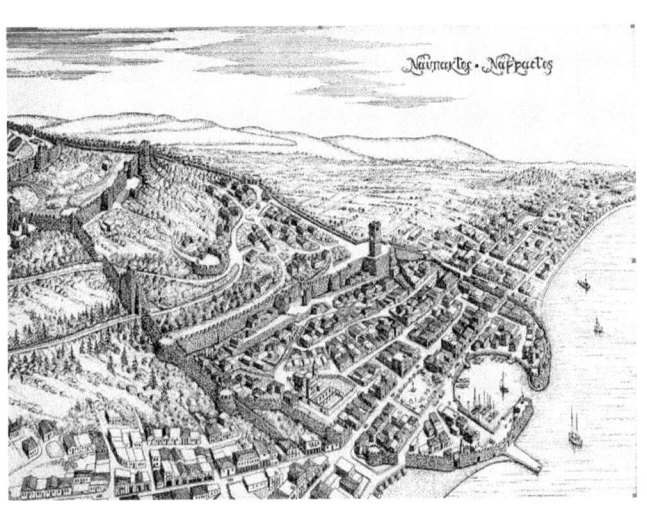

SHE FOLLOWS ME.

She follows me through all the cities I have traced through.
Or nestled within.
I am almost certain of it.

Then again
(now I finally pause to think the matter through)
it may be *she* who believes that I am in pursuit of her.
Slowly. Elliptically.

Neither of us can be sure, at least until we speak.
And even then . . .

A mutual stalking.
A feigned indifference.
A double helix.
Siamese seduction.

The same searching eyes, set inside a carnivale of masks.

OCCASIONALLY THIS GAME.

Occasionally this game overlaps, and our shadows touch.

In one city we sit face to face on a bullet train, pretending to read. Its velocity such that the world outside has frozen into pure abstraction. Cherry-hued bruises explode and remain, like scientific ink, trapped under glass.

In another city we share an elevator in silence. We are inside a building constructed by the progeny of Abraham, almost as tall as the Tower of Babel. Today is dedicated to pious observance, meaning that the elevator stops at every floor of its own accord. It is wired and programmed according to the Divine Engineer's strict instructions, opening and closing to allow invisible souls to board and disembark as they so choose, and without lifting a finger.

Despite being the only tightly coiled mortals in sight, we say nothing.

Try to breathe inaudibly.

First to step off loses.

But if we both ride to the top, the game is over.

MATTERING MAPS.

"Mattering maps" is a concept bequeathed to us by urban anthropologists, in love with their daily songlines tracing bookshop, café, home, and office. The notion is one we can all relate to. There are official maps of the city for different purposes: road maps, sewage maps, drainage maps, pollution maps, heat maps, and so on. But we all carry in our heads the personalized Baedeker of things that matter to us: shopping maps, eating maps, browsing maps, narcotic maps, erotic maps. Some corners of the city make us anxious, others curious, and still others strangely empty. Some streets are full of ghosts, while others are disturbing in their sheer inability to haunt. Anarchic romantics have suggested putting up plaques to commemorate personal landmarks and milestones: "May 22, 1995: spoke for the last time with Anna on this bench," or "July 10, 1979: broke my wrist on this step skateboarding," or "April 12, 1984: first kiss in this playground." And now the corporations follow suit.

No doubt this kind of mattering map has its charm—speaking to those fleeting, individual moments to which the city seems indifferent, and yet encourages through its very folds and concrete glades. "I stared down at this dusty necklace, the debris of a thousand automobile accidents. Within fifty years, as more and more cars collided here, the glass fragments would form a sizable bar, within thirty years a beach of sharp crystal. A new race of beachcombers might appear, squatting on these heaps of fractured windshields, sifting them for cigarette butts, spent condoms, and loose coins. Buried beneath this new geological layer laid down by the age of the automobile accident would be my own small death, as anonymous as a vitrified scar in a fossil tree."

But beyond the *dérive*, and beyond the *flâneur*, I can picture another kind of mattering map. A map that *generates* territory, rather than the other way around. Not as simulacra, but as affective blueprint. A map that does not *represent* cities that exist independently, but a map that *brings cities into being*, turning their potential and promise into brute *matter*. (But why "brute"? Matter can be as sensitive and flexible as the concepts which patronize it. And why do these concepts patronize matter? *For its insistence on being something rather than nothing.*)

Matter *matters*. That's what the drone of the city tells us.

And yet we dream of something beyond these invisible walls.

MATERIAL GIRLS.

Material girls of the world congregate here. They make pilgrimages. They see it first on TV, and then they pawn their TVs to see it firsthand. It is just as they imagined, only sweatier, and smellier, and even more intoxicating. "Oh, the mansions, the lights, the perfume, the loaded boudoirs and tables! New York must be filled with such bowers, or the beautiful, insolent, supercilious creatures could not be. Some hothouses held them."

To call someone "materialistic" once inferred that they lacked soul, and thus revered (mere) *things* over ideas and ideals. The pendulum has swung, however, so that those who care about *actual lives* proudly evoke materialism, whereas those obsessed with labels don't care whether these labels are attached to anything or not. The more evanescent the commodity, the more bowel-clutching the desire for it. The more effervescent the object, the more focused the fetish.

Which is why these girls drape themselves in tiny wisps of material in the summer, barely enough to constitute a handkerchief in the 1940s. Perversely, these whispered gestures towards dresses are in direct inverse ratio to the giant sunglasses that perch on their flint-like cheekbones. To be barely there: the ultimate fashion statement.

Blow-flies giving blow-jobs to blow-hards.

SHE LOOKS DIFFERENT.

She looks different every time I see her. And yet the recognition is swift. I wish I could say with confidence why that is, for the continuity is not of the visible world. It is a knowledge that bypasses the mind.

She has started to leave me telegraphic messages, wedged under stones in dried up birdbaths. The technique is novel: tearing out pages from old books—travel books, cook books, potboilers, catalogs—and circling the significant words in a linear fashion. Stringing these together, I wonder if she is trying to tell me of her fatigue with all this motion, her disenchantment with asymptotes and arabesques.

Every . . . body . . . continues . . . in . . . its . . . state . . . of . . . rest . . . or . . . of . . . uniform . . . motion . . . in . . . a . . . straight . . . line . . . unless . . . it . . . is . . . compelled . . . to . . . change . . . that . . . state . . . by . . . forces . . . impressed . . . upon . . . it.

(Each word circled in a coffee-stained treatise on a pioneering photographer I had never heard of . . . but why not tear out a page of Newton directly?)

I try to imagine the kind of abode she would settle for and live in. I picture views out the window of a city I have not yet seen. A prickly affair, to find oneself on the wrong side of "the topography of our intimate being." A wedding portrait, prominently displayed, perhaps. A view of a famous skyscraper from the deck. A kitchen worthy of a budding chef. And a bed boasting coils strong enough to take the strain.

"The sheltered being gives perceptible limits to her shelter. She experiences the house in its reality and in its virtuality, by means of thought and dreams. . . it is our first universe, a real cosmos in every sense of the word."

GILLES TREHIN.

Gilles Trehin lives near Nice, in the South of France. However, he spends most of his time in the city of Urville: a megalopolis which exists only inside the autistic spirals of his obsessive imagination (as well as the many drawings he has made of this fanciful polis). Urville has been expanding—as the population figures Monsieur Trehin adjusts every year attests—and boasts many impressive buildings and landmarks, such as the Place des Troubadours, the Radio-Television Métropolitaine, the Centre International des Cultures, and the Quartier des Tégartines.

Upon discovering Urville, one's first instinct is to be captivated by the detail of the place. Every suburb, every municipal building, every park, and every street has been seemingly mapped as intricately as any of the world's major metropolitan centers. The fact that the inhabitants are invisible to us adds a kind of magic. But is this really so charming for M. Trehin? I wonder if he wakes up at night, sweating and confused—the overburdened mayor to a city that itself never sleeps. Does he delegate negotiations between the preservationists and the developers, or does he take on that thankless task himself?

I BELIEVE I HAVE AN INKLING.

I believe I have an inkling of how M. Trehin feels. For while I do not claim to be the architect-deity of Napoli, I *do* spend much of my mental life there. Here I inhabit a different, much less harried life. There is a villa, to be sure, a bit worse for wear, but all the more romantic for it. There is a literary project to take seriously, and also to joyfully ignore for deep pockets of time. But most importantly, there is a beautiful and enigmatic stowaway in my midst, here on the balcony—wearing my misbuttoned shirt, and little else— munching on breadsticks with lips as red and bittersweet as pomegranate seeds.

A SERIES OF PHOTOGRAPHS.

A series of photographs of people sleeping. Sleeping in subway cars. Sleeping on benches. Sleeping at café tables. Sleeping on flattened cardboard boxes.

Title: "The City That Never Sleeps."

WRITING CAN BE.

Writing can be a form of attentiveness to the environment, and thus a rich resistance to the obligations and distractions that keep us from being mindful. Considered from this angle, it is no longer so important what the result is, in terms of "literature," but a means to maximizing one's own presence within—and connection to—the world. "What kind of tree is that?" I ask aloud.

"I don't know," a stranger replies, smiling, somewhat abashed by their own ignorance.

"Then I should find out."

WHENEVER I HAPPEN TO BE.

"Whenever I happen to be in a city of any size, I marvel that riots do not break out every day: massacres, unspeakable carnage, a doomsday chaos. How can so many human beings coexist in a space so confined without destroying each other, without hating each other to death?"

IT's So Hard.

"It's so hard to go in to the city, because you want to say 'hello' to everybody."

What Could One Possibly Do?

What could one possibly do with a key to the city?

We Spoke.

We spoke for the first time today. On the reflective deck of a giant ship, the size of a modest city.

The words were tentative. But targeted.

Like a lasso, fashioned to capture the other.

Or a rope that holds hull to wharf.

Despite hailing from elsewhere, I noticed she had the habit of young, educated Francophone women: a sharp intake of breath between sentences. As if sucking in the word "oui" backwards. This suggested to me that she had, at least once, regretted assenting to something.

There is Something.

There is something she doesn't know (or, at least, not for sure), but I can match her. Precisely. Spliced. Atom-wise.

Our trajectories, finally, began to cross in the flesh. During these encounters, in divisible cities, our bodies enjoyed both rest and motion simultaneously. Afterward, we talked of a honeymoon tour of cities that no longer exist. Constantinople. Peking. Leningrad. To name only a few.

We also speculated whether a quantum love can emerge from Euclidean spaces.

That day we discovered that sex is a kind of mapping, and bodies have—more often than not—been traversed by others. Trails have been formed. Oases rediscovered.

"Being made love to as though you inhabited someone else's sexual preferences puts you on quite complicated terms of sexual intimacy: the preferences of another body are mapped out for you on your own. So too when you are the adulterer, you make love to your lover with the pleasure (but at times, the chagrin) of unfamiliarity, mapping as you go the similarities and the differences. How can you not be comparing, measuring, playing catch-up, but still invariably registering the absent presence of another very familiar body, the one that shares your bed when you finally return to the domestic fold, for sleep if nothing else."

If love is blind, then sex is Braille.

TELESYMBIOSIS.

Telesymbiosis is defined by evolutionary biologists as "symbiosis at a distance." (And not, as I initially thought, an existential fusion with one's television set.) The mechanism for this miraculous feat is still obscure, but such a possibility is indispensible for those who subscribe to the Gaia hypothesis: the theory that the Earth somehow synchronizes its various spheres (bio-, litho-, atmo-, cryo-, hydro-) into a state of relative homeostasis. Thus, telesymbiosis puts the *stasis* in *home*, or vice versa.

Of course, estranged lovers live in a perpetual state of telesymbiosis. And each day is lived in fear of the loss of remote control.

THE PLEDGE WAS MADE.

The next morning I found another one of her notes, placed where her soft-scented body should have been. The page had been torn from an antiquated rule-book, explaining the subtleties and strategies of Chess. Only two words were circled on this occasion: "stale mate."

GILLES TREHIN.

Gilles Trehin's imagined city blooms from the monomaniacal roots of his autistic-savant mind. The cities she and I traverse—or become caught on, like a coat on a nail—lack the singular vision of Urville. Unless we are all citizens of some autistic deity's synaptic polis.

MARRIAGE.

"Marriage," I once read, "is two different people suffering from the same multiple personality disorder."

Alternatively, it is "autism for two."

Depending on one's vantage point, this is a reason to consider it, or an incentive to refuse. The persistent gnawings of loneliness, however, tend to follow the solitary traveler, like a stamp in his or her passport. And this leads to phantasies of proposals in the snow, or amongst the hibiscus. When I am awake, she says 'yes.' When I am asleep, she says 'no.'

And when I am somewhere inbetween, she simply stares back at me, uncomprehending.

DIVORCE OFTEN.

Divorce often grows within a marriage, like a cancer. Alternatively, it arrives externally, like a hit-and-run accident. One should never rush to judgment, though, given that not all marriages are healthy or pleasant. Divorce, of course, in this case can be a liberation. But the fact remains that two people pledged eternal love, but sooner or later realized the futility—perhaps even arrogance—of attempting to stretch an emotion, born within a specific and exacting set of circumstances, from one year to the next to the next and so on. Emotions, like everything else, become frayed over time. Impassioned commitments lose their vibrant colors, just as the circuits of habit cut deeper and deeper into the heart over time.

The saddest expression of this, like catching one's soul on a nail, comes precisely 48 minutes into Dziga Vertov's celebrated avant-garde documentary film of 1929, *Man With a Movie Camera*. This kinetic man and his *kino-apparatum* happen to cross paths with a defeated couple in Odessa, waiting for the paperwork of their divorce to be handed over. Whether it was previously a happy marriage or not matters little when we see the woman's brief but haunting expression. She is ashamed. She is heartsick. She is divorced.

"To breed an animal that is entitled to make promises—surely that is the essence of the paradoxical task nature has set itself where human beings are concerned? Isn't that the real problem of human beings?"

When Does a Town?

When does a town become a city? Can we measure it by population? If so, should we take the minimum to be a million souls? Let's say, for the sake of a thought experiment, we can. In which case, neither Geneva, nor Amsterdam, qualify as a city. Which leaves us with the original conundrum. What criteria do we use to distinguish a town from a city? Or a metropolis from a megalopolis? I have no tools, save intuition.

In Geneva, everything depends on the quality of light. On certain mornings and evenings, the surrounding mountains appear to be marching on the city—a giant golden slab, which an extended palm could almost touch. At other times, the granite withdraws to become a remote façade, like a painted movie set. France itself is a tide that ebbs and flows, lapping at the shores of Lac Leman.

No Sighting of Her.

No sighting of her for several months. It is almost a relief. I can knuckle down. Stop looking over my shoulder. There is work to be done.

Every now and then I lose resolve, and walk out of my way to the city's (or town's) main mailing center. Then I go to the *poste restante* desk. But there is nothing waiting for me. How could there be? Names, addresses, are mutually unknown. At least, if they were, they have since changed.

As good as a holiday, they say. But as already indicated, I have come here to work. And so a bristling mood pushes her to the margins of my mind.

ONCE A YEAR.

Once a year, the good people of Geneva test their sirens, stirring up a swarm of sleep-angry hornets from their sticky slumber. Perhaps the Germans are advancing over the frosted Alps, or Zurich has finally declared war on this ancient and stubborn republic.

On these occasions, the yodels of war match the steel epiglottis of the sirens, draped over these erratic rocks. Perhaps the enemy is now within these flaming tunnels, like a vasectomy gone wrong. It must be a sign: planes falling out of the sky, and bringing their stock prices with them. Or a disgruntled bus driver who turns the local council-chambers into an abattoir.

Then again, the enemy may in fact be the drug dealers down in the *jardin d'anglais*, who address potential customers in Arab-accented French, initially formal, and then less so, *Cherchez-vous, monsieur?* . . . the pavement one long spittoon. Or perhaps these sirens wail against the boredom that clings to the breath like fog, even in the summer, when the flamers and the families splay their hairy wares at the *bains de Paquis* for all to see (presuming you are looking). Or even the squatters—squatting—releasing black, tacky, hemp-colored turds over their docile neighbors every Saturday night. Future bank-tellers blowing off steam. Multilingual, yet monocultural. Both homogenized and pasteurized. Blank as a blanket of fresh snow, awaiting the steaming yellow signature of Brussels.

Geneva seems most calm for a town surrounded. A tiny red-and-white island circled by a sea of blue-and-yellow. Whether they acknowledge it openly or not, the rest of Europe is closing in.

Advancing on a people who see no shame concerning intoxication through cheese.

LIKE GENEVA.

Like Geneva, Amsterdam can seem like a different place, depending on the quality of light. Few scenes are more picturesque than the dilated reflections on the dancing, drunk buildings, stretching and bouncing off the mellow, glittering canals. Every window acts as a prism for fractured rainbows, errant sparklers, and undulating will-o-the-wisps. To the tourist, this is the essential charm of the city (town?)—the way the sun is a composed companion, never threatening to turn one's skin an angry pink. It is a golden pool for Vermeer to dip his ladle, and pour over the canvas, sloping softly down the tiny bridges and alleyways. For the resident, however, these idyllic and seemingly endless summer evenings are the fleeting flipside of the bleakness which molds the soul for nine months of the year.

Rain that never stops, and comes at impossible angles. The storms of the North Sea, which care little for the sober and arrogant men who, through sheer stubborn will, built a landmass, and then a country here. Men and women who walk on water, droplets all the while beading on orange plastic-lacquered skin, a genetic inheritance which allows all-year shopping expeditions by rusted bicycle. A brood of children in a bucket lashed to the handlebars, who have not yet heard the name Calvin, but are already stunted by his constipated notions, from the inside.

"So how do you like it here?" I asked my new neighbor, from Berlin, as much out of politeness as curiosity.

"Sometimes I want to smash the window, and cut my face with the glass," she replied, without the hint of a smile.

The Great Painters.

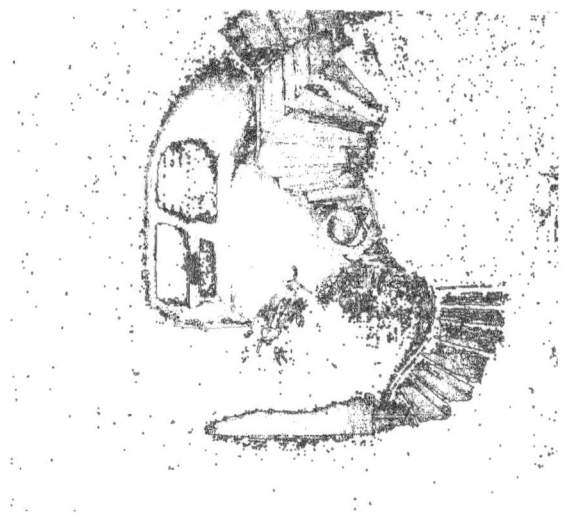

The great painters of the lowlands tell us much about Amsterdam before electricity. Here, the saturated citizens coveted light more than gold, for they had plenty of the latter. Surely they huddled around Rembrandt's canvas as one would around a bonfire. A miraculous warmth for the eyes, amidst the musty smell of sackcloth.

WALTER BURLEY GRIFFIN.

Walter Burley Griffin shares something in common with Guy Trehin, in that he is an architect-deity. However, Burley Griffin's town
(pop. 309,500) did not die with him, trapped in the folded grey
topography of his mind, but continues to this day, after leaping
from the drafting table into the blinding Australian sunlight. Canberra, allegedly an Aboriginal word for "meeting place," was
established after an international design competition in 1911. This
had been arranged by the fledgling Australian Federation, having
decided on a site diplomatically removed from both Sydney and
Melbourne, nestled in "an amphitheatre of hills." Because Australia
was so remote from those with the expertise to design a new city,
interested parties received detailed information kits, and soon

enough 137 different visions for Canberra were exhibited to the public. After the usual wrangling, Burley Griffin, a young man from Chicago, emerged the winner. At the time, many believed this was due to his prominent architectural connections, including Frank Lloyd Wright himself. It is understood today, however, that the exquisite drawings by his wife, Marion Mahony Griffin, tipped the balance in his favor.

And so, a meeting place was established for politicians and diplomats, academics and bureaucrats, journalists and plutocrats, as well as the many service industries which spring up to service an elite which had somewhat gone to seed. What has been called "the crisis of achieved utopia" manifested itself in a suburban sprawl, pock-marked by roundabouts and rifle ranges. There are still tiny slivers of the "bush capital," such as the Carillion, in which one can detect the echo of Burley Griffin's intentions: a naïve faith in New World progress, and the refined aesthetics of Corbusian social engineering. But less than a century into its short life, Canberra is choked by the toxic weeds of boredom, futility, and asymptotic superannuation. A giant hypodermic needle, known as the Telecom Tower, dominates the skyline, reminding all under its shadow that heroin use is rampant among the middle-class. And while the parliamentarians debate the merits of apologizing to whomever is left of the indigenous population, kangaroo carcasses litter the roadsides.

Legend Has It.

Legend has it that Rome, the Eternal City, was founded by two brothers, Romulus and Remus, suckled and nurtured by a proud she-wolf. Canberra, in contrast, was founded by the Federal Capital Advisory Committee, under one Mr. John Sulman.

THE CAPTAIN COOK WATER-FOUNTAIN.

The Captain Cook Water-Fountain, displayed prominently in the artificial lake named after Burley Griffin, is an exact replica of Geneva's *jet d'eau*, sending an unimaginative plume of water five hundred feet into the sky, for no other reason than somebody figured out the hydraulic means to do so. Two Swiss engineers were brought out to Australia as consultants (and one can only *imagine* the crazy shenanigans that they got up to during their trip down under).

Once, for a dare when I was about twelve, I foolishly steered a paddleboat under this fountain, and immediately regretted it. Each gigantic drop felt like an avalanche of rocks, and I seemed to be trapped under this merciless pummeling for an eternity, no matter how hard my skinny legs paddled. (I now know that this fountain pumps six tons of water in the air at any given moment.) On the way back to my father's office, my squelching sneakers left a trail on the baking footpath, and I received a tongue-lashing once I got there for the incongruous sin of being both damp and dressed.

This partly explains why it was such a clammy and uncanny moment to see the *jet d'eau* on my first day after moving to Switzerland. I had no idea that Geneva and Canberra were synchronicities. And yet it makes perfect sense. Both are based around lakes. Both are centers of government and administration. And both boast hubristic water features that function as symbolic enemas for their docile populace.

GLOBALLY SPEAKING.

Globally speaking, Australians are everywhere, but Australia is nowhere.

WERE I.

Were I an architect-deity, I would create an Escheresque subway system linking all the cities in the world. The tunnels themselves, and the people decanted from one place to the other, would eventually create an Ecumenopolis: a single and continuous city, enlaced and endless. Were this the case I could get on the F train at Delancey Street, Manhattan, and—after a couple of changes midtown—emerge in the night-markets of Taipei, or near the Roman baths of Budapest. Or perhaps even downtown Urville.

IT'S NOT UNCOMMON.

It's not uncommon to see "mutton dressed as lamb." But in Geneva, you often see carcass dressed as mutton. Quite unnerving, really. Clearly this country, dedicated to all things related to the passing of time, has an interesting attitude to the ageing process. Ironic, also, that the Swiss are famous for the clocks and watches that they make in order to measure just how slow time passes in this painfully dull place.

Take, for instance, the sign in English affixed to my local hair-dresser's window: "Select a style from our new range of *shocking* haircuts." This is funny the first dozen times I pass it on my way to work, but then loses its flavor.

When I get to the office, my boss quotes Dostoevsky's diary: "Been in Geneva a week. The perfect place to commit suicide."

WHILE WAITING.

While waiting in airports I like to amuse myself by composing brief lists of oxymorons. These come to me almost unbeckoned: a useless facility, which nevertheless manages to fill time. I scribble some new entries next to those already in my notebook: "wise fool," "diet coke," "military intelligence," "social science," "delicious marzipan," "cotton wool," "happily married," "domestic bliss," "good parent," "humble opinion," "human nature," "friendly fire," "emotional maturity," "sexy girdle," "obscene caller," "Fox News," "legitimate source," and "correct choice."

These I then wed to tautologies, in a mental word jumble that, depending on the level of my jet-lag, either looks like a professional game of Scrabble, or a bowl of spilled alphabet soup. Some such pleonasms include: "vanity publishing," "social obligation," "English homosexual," "unreliable narrator," "cybernetic organism," "ulterior motive," "human error," "nervous system," "false advertising," "merry widow," "meaningless sex," "impossible love," "libidinal economy," "sexual tension," and—of course—"scam artist."

In the Retro-Futuristic Film.

In the retro-futuristic film *Rollerball*, all the world's books have been taken to a giant database in Geneva. All other cities have to make do with corporate summaries of books, transcribed by computer. Looking at the placid mania raging around me, this dystopian conceit doesn't seem too implausible.

On the whole, the locals speak the universal language: "lingua franc" (or euro, or dollar).

Yet ultimately, "the Alpine lands, home of the toy and the funicular, the merry-go-round and the thin chime, were not a being *here*, as in France, with French vines growing over one's feet on the ground."

THE RHÔNE.

The Rhône is one of my few friends here. It seems the only other entity in a hurry to be elsewhere. To get the hell away.

"The main forces of the thunderstorm remained massed down the Rhône valley as if loath to attack the respectable and passionless abode of democratic liberty, the serious-minded town of dreary hotels, tendering the same indifferent hospitality to tourists of all nations and to international conspirators of every shade."

"The trouble with the Rhône is that it is, finally, too *obvious*—it is the sort of river that might be designed by a conscientious tourist board."

"On the centre of the lake, cooled by the piercing current of the Rhône, lay the true centre of the Western World. Upon it floated swans like boats and boats like swans, both lost in the nothingness of the heartless beauty."

Even this city's most famous son, Jean-Jacques Rousseau, is on record as saying, "as to returning to Geneva, it never entered into my imagination."

I Have no Country.

"I have no country. And the more I see of countries, the more I like the idea."

Moving Four Blocks.

Moving four blocks in New York City can mean moving between countries. When I changed apartments from Rivington Street to Grand Street, this didn't seem like a big change, geographically speaking (since I would still be using the Delancey subway stop). Culturally speaking, however, this was a massive shift. Whereas before I was living in the rowdy, music-filled streets of Puerto Rico, I now found myself housed in a much more sedate Central European enclave. Out my study window I could see China, which itself has all but colonized Italy. No doubt my next move will be South East, across the river; despite the fact that living in Brooklyn is like marrying the most exciting woman in the world, and then sleeping in the next room.

IT SEEMS.

It seems she has given me the pink slip, as it were.

WALKING.

Walking to breakfast early on a Sunday morning, I was struck by the sound of birdsong in Sara D. Roosevelt Park: a strip of green between the blight of the Bowery and Allen Street. Here, hanging from the branches of trees and bushes were three dozen birdcages, most far too small for the ornithological specimens hopping around inside. Many were draped in light canvas, which did little to muffle the polyphonic din. The old, wiry Chinese men, clustered in groups nearby, seemed to find this conference of birds soothing. If it was an actual bird market, like the one I had seen a few years earlier in Kowloon, I did not notice anyone anxious to make a sale. Perhaps each cage belonged to one of the men, and they come down here every weekend in some time-honored Confucian ritual. To oversee a parliament of fowls.

I watch the birds for a while, but there is no deeper metaphor to be gleaned. I have no idea why the caged birds sing.

But I *am* convinced that our mattering maps are now mashups of the whole world. Implosion is indeed the dominant logic of our time.

Is Anyone Else.

"Is anyone else being woken by the robin that is singing before dawn? If so, please contact me by phone or email, so we can arrange for management to deal with this problem."

So reads the rather ominous flyer plastered near the elevators in my new apartment building. First Afghanistan. Then Iraq. Now this. We are in the middle of Manhattan, and people are freaked out—tormented, even—by the tiny flecks of nature still perched on this island.

THE ENTIRE BAR.

The entire bar is watching intently by now. Two young men seem to be breaking some kind of local record by constructing a table-tower—the Jenga equivalent of the Shanghai Bank building. Bad *feng-shui* or not, the room is getting pretty excited. One player is noticeably jumpy, hopping triumphantly about the room whenever he successfully extracts a wooden brick, placing it delicately on the top of the wobbling structure. The other guy is more collected, sucking on a cigarette and keeping a poker face throughout the tense contest. For at least fifteen minutes it is impossible to get a drink, since the two bar-girls, tiny women in giant shoes and spiky haircuts, are entranced by this latest challenge to Hong Kong's besieged gravity.

I am the only *gwailo* in the place, and the two players periodically glance in my direction and nod, to which I mime some kind of Esperanto encouragement, or roll my eyes in exaggerated antici-pation of catastrophe. It is uncanny to me how similar this Jenga-spire looked to the ubiquitous high-rises which cram Hong Kong's harbor.

Then, inevitably breaking the Canto-pop-infused tension with a crash, the tower comes tumbling down . . .

Since returning from a week in Hong Kong I've been having a recurrent dream. I'm walking around the crowded streets, hopping onto escalators, getting into lifts, hanging on to cable cars and mar-ching along twisting flyovers. I don't know where I'm trying to get to, but I definitely have to keep moving. Otherwise I'll end up like that old man I saw, stuffed into a tiny wooden booth and buried in broken shoes. Maybe sleeping, maybe suffocated.

The heat is truly astonishing, broiling me like those black tea eggs in giant baskets on the sidewalk. Periodically, I pass a major buil-ding that blasts frozen, reconstituted air out of its orifices, only serving to warp the body's internal thermostat. I seem to be going in circles, looking for the giant mall that will eventually lead me back to the hotel. (Perhaps Fredric Jameson had a point after all, and wasn't just a toasted academic staggering around the Westin Bonaventure Hotel trying to find his room.) It seems, however, that I took a wrong turn somewhere, and am now on the longest escalator in the world, heading up toward Victoria Peak. This escalator is outdoors, and reversed depending on the direction of rush hour.

THERE IS AN ESSENTIAL DIFFERENCE.

There is an essential difference between a city located on a lake and those based around harbors. Likewise, a city perched on top of a flowing river, away from the coast, is influenced by alternate aquatic forces. I have heard it said that lake cities are best for contemplation, while those near the sea provoke the passions, but can't vouch for sure, even though I have lived in both. Does it make any difference if the lake is "manmade," as it is in Canberra? And what if the sea has been engineered into submission, as it has in Amsterdam?

Canberra, Geneva, and Chicago have this much in common: the subconscious knowledge that were one needful of escape by boat, then there is a finite distance one can cover before running out of water. They are contained. In contrast, Paris, London, and Rome—while land-locked—can access the sea via the Seine, Thames, and Tiber.

New York, of course, is based on a harbor, but serves as the destination for many of the world's escapees, not the point of origin. One must entertain the possibility, however, that during this now endless state of exception, the tide is perhaps slowly turning.

On one particularly stormy weekend, Canberra's main cemetery was flooded. This, combined with the effects of soil erosion, sent a flotilla of coffins into Lake Burley Griffin. I imagined this disturbed several people in paddleboats that day.

I Seem to Be.

I seem to be on the street again, taking another wrong turn, and finding myself in Chungking Mansions, a festering warren that I vaguely know by cinematic proxy. It seems to be the most literal incarnation of a tourist trap I've ever encountered, with labyrinthine twists and turns promising escape, but only beckoning fools further into the steamy center of the beast. Dead rats, used tampons, and rotting fruit are crammed into corners and onto stairwells, while the fire escape doors are nailed shut. It is surely only a matter of time before this architectural delirium is razed like the infamous Walled City—also in Kowloon—which boasted a population density equivalent to three million people per square mile. I duck between two stalls and emerge into a dark alleyway. Some young ne'er-do-wells are sitting around patiently, like fishermen, and when they see me they spring into action, running toward me and shouting. They're probably just pimps or hawkers, but I hightail it out of there anyway. Just in case.

A week after I leave Hong Kong, physically at least, a massive typhoon hits the harbor. Boats are tossed across piers, cranes thrown off buildings, and bamboo scaffolding launched into the air like a thousand javelins. Many of its famous skyscrapers have their windows blown out by the pressure, and a China Airlines jet flips on to its back as it tries to land on the tarmac.

Seeing these images on the news prompts me to remember (or dream) the laughter in the pub as the Jenga tower crashes to the table. The girls say something cheeky and then return to work. The guys take a long swig of beer and compare shaky hands. Then they scoop the scattered tiles into a pile and started again.

THE F TRAIN.

The F train is arguably the most iconic of New York's subway lines, not least because it threads the three high-profile boroughs of Brooklyn, Manhattan and Queens. Not only that, but the F links two significant origin sites of the media spectacle: Coney Island and the 1964 World's Fair. The former was one of the launchpads for modernism, while the latter (it could be argued), helped inaugurate postmodernism.

Something the V train, the F's poor, surly—and now discontinued—cousin, could never claim.

SHE AND I.

She and I both suffer from Garbo syndrome. To want to be alone, but to have one's absence sorely missed.

I MET.

I met a collector of grace. An old, frail gentleman, who had each encounter cataloged in his mind, painted in mnemonic brushstrokes on the inside of his eyelids. An elbow here. An eyelash there. A silhouette. A hesitation. A blush. A certain stoop to talk to a child. The minute movement of the mouth, registering a monumental internal decision. And yet he claimed none of these belonged to the body which expressed it. Grace, for him, was a trick of the light, like a fragment of rainbow, created by a prism. Take away the radiant source, however, and one is left with transparent crystal. On this point I felt I should disagree. But held my tongue.

NEW YORK IS NOT REALLY.

"New York is not really part of America," everyone says. It's not really America but a foreign land. New Yorkers will tell you this, and so too will 'mainlanders,' the former with resignation, the latter with resentment. But perhaps it is really the other way around. New York is all that's left of the real America."

An interesting idea. In any case, I cannot help but feel that this city is being destroyed by too many immigrants. That is to say, by those affluent refugees from the mainland. Pamperers of pug-dogs. Pushers of Bugaboos. Swillers of skinny lattés. Soft-boiled potato people, bringing a blithe sense of entitlement in their wake.

A statistic: the average salary of a white family in Manhattan in 2007 is $300,000. The conditions are ripe for a new Terror, aimed at the inhabitants of these Versailles-in-the-Sky, as well as those who cower in its shadows.

Pristine guillotines fly through the air.

REUNION.

Reunion is the wrong word. That suggests there was a "union" in the first place. Rather a recollision.

We lie in the fragrant wreckage of tangled limbs and damp high thread counts: the bloodgates opened internally.

While I am still trying to figure out if it is really *her*, she tells me she wants to make an open promise. Not to promise anything in particular, that is, but simply to make a pure promise. A promise to promise whatever I might insist upon in the future. A signed blank check on which a figure would be traced at a time of my choosing, and according to a value my self of many morrows might ascribe.

This is either the most precious gift I have ever received, or the romantic equivalent of that old business mantra, "the check is in the mail."

RECENTLY I SPENT.

Recently I spent at least twenty minutes trying to explain the difference between "middle America" and "Central America" to my Japanese friend, Koichi. Whether I really succeeded or not is an open question complicated by the fact that there are middle Americans in Central America (tourists), and Central Americans in middle America (immigrants).

Moves are afoot to build a giant wall between the US and Mexico. Only one more reason to invest in a t-shirt spotted in the Lower East Side: "USA out of NYC."

ON JANUARY 22, 2006.

On January 22, 2006, the roof of the First Roumanian American Synagogue on Rivington Street collapsed. Whether the rumors were true or not—that the congregation had allowed it to fall into such a state of disrepair in order to sell the now lucrative property—this holy site was left exposed for more than a month. It was exposed to the elements, and to the prying eyes of people walking by, as city officials argued who was responsible for demolition and removal. Everything was left untouched, so anyone across the street could see the candelabras, the pews, the stained-glass windows, all waiting in the rain for a ceremony which had been infinitely postponed. The sacred spilled onto the curb like a pile of bricks, leaking out into the profane and unsettling those who prefer their religious spaces to be hidden from view. "I don't care what they do, as long as I don't have to see it."

One could be forgiven for thinking that God himself had lifted the roof like the lid of a saucepan, or the top of a cupcake.

Twenty-one People.

Twenty-one people lost their lives in 1919, when a ninety-by-fifty-foot tank filled with hot molasses, and located in the heart of Boston, finally burst its walls. The owners of this tank were well aware of this possible calamity, since they had painted the exterior brown, in order to hide the many leaks. Kids and dogs often burnt their curious tongues, but still the dubious operation continued. One day, the pressure became too much, and a lava flow of liquid sugar suddenly extinguished many lives, and injured dozens of others.

Reading about this anachronistic industrial disaster, I find myself wondering if this is where the phrase "sticky end" came from.

No Two People.

No two people visit the same city. Perception and judgment depend not only on the light or the season, but the company, the neighborhood, the footwear, the bank balance, the blood-sugar count, the police-tape, the languages acquired, the guidebooks consulted, and an infinite number of other contingencies and variables. And so we are in the realm of chalk and cheese when discussing cities. "Oh, you didn't like Amsterdam? It's my favorite city." "Oh, you found Beijing dull? I must say that sounds preposterous." Etc.

As for myself, I wonder if I moved to New York because my subconscious shepherded me toward one of my earliest dwelling places: the stoops of *Sesame Street*.

I Have Heard Word.

I have heard word that she is in Tokyo, albeit only briefly. I picture her in the window seat of a JAL jumbo jet, pensively pushing her cuticles and waiting for the Xanax to kick in. If she presses her forehead against the window, she can see the ground staff, lining up and bowing low as the plane taxis away from the gate.

"Melancholy," she once said, "is the state of affairs."

To be a harem of one. A destiny of sorts.

FILM ALLOWS US.

Film allows us to linger in cities before we have actually had the opportunity to travel there. Oftentimes this is no doubt the least risky way to experience them, as is certainly the case with *City of God*. I don't think a single feature film has yet been made which uses Canberra as a backdrop, which is a shame, for alienation has rarely been rendered so methodically, and in such concrete terms. Geneva was the location for Kieslowski's *Three Colors: Red*, although that's the extent of my knowledge on the subject. I imagine there are others, but the fact that they don't come readily to mind is significant. The great Harold Lloyd used the early megastores of Chicago for some of the most memorable scenes in silent cinema. While Paris and Rome, of course, have played the muse for generations of auteurs.

It is safe to say, however, that *everyone* who has seen a film or a TV show, has lived in New York City, at least for a while. And perhaps this accounts for the variety of people here, since many come here seeking different versions of the place that they have seen on the screen. How to reconcile *The Warriors* with *Sesame Street*? *Naked City* with *Top Hat*? *Westside Story* with Batman's Gotham? Woody Allen with Spike Lee? Andy Warhol with *Friends*? And even within Martin Scorsese's output, we have Edith Wharton's genteel brownstones juxtaposed with Travis Bickle's squalid apartment, as well as 19th-century Battery Park gangs, and *After Hours*' darkly hilarious portrait of 1980s SoHo.

WE CAN TRACE.

We can trace the dotted line back to the proto-cinematic magic of the old mutoscopes, a feature of Coney Island boardwalk more than a century ago, with titles such as "What the Butler Saw" and "Birth of the Pearl." Reminding us that the voyeuristic impulse—watching intently—creates the same illusion as closing one's eyes. Specifically, that one is invisible.

An Uncomfortable Thought.

An uncomfortable thought: that your eyes never stop staring. That even if you close your eyelids, your pupils are still boring into the back of the thin, tender skin. Constantly swiveling and seeking, the oracular orbs indulge their insatiable appetite for images. A desperate search for the imprint of light on retina. Even after the other organs have ceased to function, perhaps. The eyes still staring. Registering the scene before them, without a brain or memory to record it. A camera without film. Even after the living gently close the eyelids, in respect for the dead.

THE NAME OF GOTHAM CITY.

The name of Gotham City can be traced to Washington Irving's 1807 work, *Salmagundi*. As far back as the 15th century; however, the sobriquet of "Gotham" had been used to refer to "places with foolish inhabitants."

NOWADAYS.

Nowadays, due to the prohibitive costs of filming in Irving's metropolis, Gotham on screen can be a digital fusion of New York City and Chicago. This is what allows the El train to rumble above ground, and snake its way between the Chrysler building and Grand Central Station, in defiance of both realty and reality. In my mind's eye, it takes a concerted effort to extricate one skyline from the other.

IT IS IN CHICAGO.

It is in Chicago that one can experience the surreal site of prisoners, dressed in orange overalls, looking down on the free folk, as the latter go about their business downtown. The recreational facility of this prison is a barred roof, thirty stories into the sky. Here the inmates presumably smoke and talk and spit on, as well as dream of being, one of the anonymous ants that scurry along Printer's Row: a neighborhood famous for its history of publishing and procurement. (Here the sons of Gutenberg came to press the flesh.)

An interesting corrective technique. To give the criminal a bird's eye view of that which they are denied. An absurd observatory, creating tourists held hostage in a Brunelleschian canvas. There is a sadism here, too. Allowing the prisoners to watch the storms roll in, yet barring them from sharing the muffled, rye-flavored solidarity of the locals, against the common enemy of February lake effects.

In a Chicago winter, the chattering of teeth suffices for small talk.

BETWEEN HERE AND THERE.

Between here and there, it would take two hours on a plane, twelve hours on a train, perhaps six days on a Segway, and several weeks on foot. The weather comes from there and arrives here a day later. A day after she has experienced it. It is second-hand weather. Pre-loved or pre-loathed, depending on the forecast. Sometimes, I believe I can scent her presence in the rain, and divine yesterday's cooking in the sun-bleached breeze.

And yet, *here* is an hour ahead of *there*. So the paradox is this: Time occurs here first, while actual events (i.e., the weather) occur there first. I fear I need more than a scientist to explain this to me. It is an enigma beyond the geophysical spider-webs spun from the astral-arachnid body of Greenwich observatory. It is beyond the Delphic banality of meteorology.

The answer, I suspect, is neither here nor there.

In which case it would be . . . *where*, exactly?

In 1595.

In 1595, Sir Francis Drake and his armada attempted to take the city of Maracaibo, underneath the cloak of night. His plan, however, was foiled due to almost constant flashes of lightning over Venezuela's Catatumbo River, illuminating the hostile ships, and alerting the city's defenses. Drake was thus pinned down by forks of electricity, his ambitions devoured by the perverse appetites of Fate. Even today, this lightning persists: a storm that has lasted for many centuries. Scientists continue to argue over the reasons for this atmospheric anomaly. Some say it is due to rising gases, others because of the air currents created by the Andes. But whatever the explanation, it is reliable enough to use as a navigation aid for pilots and mariners alike.

AN IMPOSSIBLE VOYAGE.

An Impossible Voyage, Georges Méliès fantastic cinematic tale of 1904, began its first screening with a live narrator, who explained the events unfolding on the screen: "Gathered to discuss the proposed voyage around the world, we meet the most influential members of the Institute of Incoherent Geography. President Paul Hunter announces the arrival of engineer Crazyloff, progenitor of a marvelous scheme. Krisiloff explains his project that will employ every known means of locomotion—railroads, automobiles, dirigible balloons, submarines, boats, etc. The institute enthusiastically votes to proceed with the unparalleled plan."

Watching a restored print of this film, in a private screening booth of an archive in Italy, I am thunderstruck by two things. First, the very notion of an Institute of Incoherent Geography. Surely I am an honorary member of such a society, if not necessarily an "influential" one. Second, *she* is somehow on screen, playing one of the ladies on the platform, stage left, as the engineer explains his ambitious plan to circumnavigate the globe.

Of course it cannot *really* be her, I tell myself. True, she has certainly been known to frequently play tricks with space. Yet I fiercely resist that notion that she can do the same with time.

Upon further reflection, I am distracted and torn. *What if this is indeed her?* Does this *increase* or *decrease* my chances of encountering her again?

WE HAD TO.

"We had to break up this aura that surrounds acts and bodies for them to be able to meet by chance in the street, concentrate in such great number in cities or camps, draw close or melt into each other in love. A very powerful force was required to break this magnetic distance where each body moves, as well as to produce this indifferent space where chance is able to put them into contact. Something of this refractory power remains in each of us, even at the heart of the modern secularized spaces, even in the use we make of our emancipated, spatially liberated bodies . . . Chance, therefore, along with the statistical probability that characterizes our modern world, are unclean and obscene modalities. Right now we must accommodate all of this in the name of freedom; one day, this refusal—this untying that makes multiple meetings possible, accelerating the Brownian movement of our lives—will return with a deadly indetermination and indifference, and overwhelm us. Chance not only tires God, it tires us too."

I ATTEMPT TO CALCULATE.

I attempt to calculate the chances of running in to her on this rickety verandah café, if I am willing to come here every day for a year. Even the philosophers are beginning to talk about destiny again, without irony. (*"Relation is already a descent into its own particles."*) Perhaps it is inscribed within one of the spilled tributaries of the Milky Way, even as the night sky slides southward with each passing orbit. For while the constellation of Crux was once visible to the Hellenic astronomers and poets of classical times, it has long since slipped under the nocturnal horizon into the lower hemisphere. That is to say, the Southern Cross was once visible in the North, suggesting even stars fall prey to a nomadic gravity, a celestial wanderlust.

SERENDIPITY.

"Serendipity," she said, her eyes widening like a child, presented with an unexpected piece of cake. "Why, that's my favorite type of dipity!"

LIKE A CODEX.

Like a codex that has been etched and erased over many generations, the city is a barely coherent palimpsest, and today's inhabitants seek their own story on the other side of celluloid. Melbourne. The anti-polis. So much less than the sum of its parts. New York. The cosmopolis. So much more.

Here we have a young woman from Russia, who laughs with giddy shame when she confesses this fact to strangers. Here a businessman, perhaps from Seoul, sitting in the park with a suit, tie and no shoes. Here a homeless man trying to give away ten dollars, much to everyone's consternation. Here a couple in their fifties, tripping on ecstasy, celebrating their first wedding anniversary. Here a young girl, wearing a Santa hat in the middle of June, trying to save a sick pigeon. And through windows, glimpses of possible lives. A violin in the early stages of repair. A bookshelf filled with the same book, over and over again. And hanging from a café stool, signs of a bachelor's life: the presumption of a toothbrush tucked in the inside pocket of his jacket.

"It's possible that in places like New York people can remain in a kind of positive, happy fluidity, a state of transpearing. But most people experience it as a kind of liquid terror."

Maybe I'm Projecting.

Maybe I'm projecting, but the pigeons in Venice seem to have more *style* than those in London, and most definitely more than those in New York. These last seem even more wretched than the junkies in Tompkins Square Park, asleep in the hot sun, on pillows of vomit. I half expect these oily, frazzled, limping pigeons to accost me as I distractedly read on a bench: "C'mon man. Spare a breadcrumb? A piece of corn?" The pigeons in Geneva, however, are plump and complacent. During sunrise and sunset they sound like throaty people, making love. (Which is fitting, given that the couples of Geneva sound like obscenely cooing pigeons when they fuck.)

NO CITY.

No city can hold a candle to Venice for sheer enchantment, for the sense that one is moving within a Gothic Persian fairytale, as narrated by Calvino. Even when one is well aware that it is an entire city built on water, to walk out of the train station onto the glittering Grand Canal, gondolas gliding North and South, is to be left breathless for several hours. Indeed, the absence of cars is just as important as the presence of watercraft, for this creates an entirely unfamiliar scene.

Venice, one of the first true republics, and only grudgingly absorbed into Italy through the frailty of age, still stands proud, even as its actual citizens flee like rats from a sinking ship. (The rats, in this case, seem in no hurry to escape, as long as there are tourists still leaving scraps in their wake.) Here, the difference between night and day is that of life and death, love and hate. Both are necessary, and both have their appeal, but issue from essentially opposed forces.

During the day, we see Venice in all its decadent elegance: crumbling, abandoned, yet still boasting a magnificent architectural fusion of East and West. In sunlight, we see "the visible form of invisibility." At night, however, bearings are quickly lost, and shadows stalk the many bridges that lead new arrivals deeper and deeper into shuttered darkness. Long boats sliding silently between buildings no longer seem romantic, but slightly sinister, with shapeless lumps of glowing tallow molded to the bow, more for comfort than light, which is sucked up thirstily by the walls.

I picture the city in a decade hence, when the streets are permanently flooded, a lone gondolier steering his craft through the giant doorway of a palace, maneuvering his way around the chandelier, whose lowest crystals now play with the surface of the lagoon like a child's fingers, testing the temperature of the water. Back in the here and now, through a high window, a woman in a carnival mask laughs at something her companion said or did. (Doesn't this shit only happen in Nicholas Roeg or Stanley Kubrick movies?)

And when the patrons of the opera house have long since floated back to their homes or hotel rooms, the pigeons line the edge of St. Marks Square, heads tucked beneath worn-velvet wings, like bashful vampires.

THEY ARE PREPARED.

"They are prepared for the strangest names—nothing can surprise them—for, as frugal as they may otherwise be in experience, in this city they nonchalantly abandon themselves to the most extravagant possibilities. In their usual existence they constantly confuse what is extraordinary with what is forbidden, so that the expectation of something marvelous, which they now permit themselves, appears on their faces as an expression of coarse licentiousness . . . . They let themselves be excited by the almost deadly confessions of music as if by physical indiscretions: so, without even beginning to master the existence of Venice, they surrender themselves to the lucrative swoon of gondolas."

I Once Met.

I once met a Polish Zen master who loved reggae. He told me of his pilgrimage to Kingston, Jamaica, and his sense that all the locals were somehow tuned into the same music. Music that outsiders could not hear. The people of Kingston walked with a shared and languid rhythm, as if the very trees and buildings were broadcasting a deep dub sonic plate from the bottom of the ocean.

This can easily be contrasted with the cacophony of New York, in which millions of people move in distinct ways to jagged, clashing, treble-heavy soundtracks.

Some aural graffiti I would like to add to the mix:

cacophony → caca phony → phony caca → bullshit

THE EXPERTS WARN US.

The experts warn us against ID theft. Credit card and social security numbers are enough information to enable one unscrupulous individual to masquerade as another. But I have yet to hear anyone caution us against the dangers of *id* theft—a more Freudian, and thus intimate, crime. Stealing a person's public persona is one thing. To steal the deepest core of their primal desires is another. And just as you may be a victim of identity theft, serenely oblivious until your bank account is empty, you may also be an unknowing victim of id theft. Only much later will you realize that your most naked impulses have been snatched from inside your most intimate hiding places, leaving only the ego and superego to coast into the future—a vehicle blessed with direction, but bereft of drive.

MUCH HAS BEEN MADE.

Much has been made of so-called "tipping points," no doubt because this phrase sounds more scientific than "turning a corner." 2006 was a momentous year in human history, because—again, according to the experts—this was the point at which the planetary balance shifted. More people now live in urban spaces than in rural or sparsely populated areas. Humanity has voted with its feet, and decided that it prefers living in the city rather than the country. (Or at least, that it has more chance of surviving in the city than in the country.)

The same year was witness to another staggering reversal: the ratio of artificial agents on the World Wide Web began to outnumber those of humans. Since 2006, there are more bots, spiders, and other AI entities probing the reaches of cyberspace than people.

Not only are the great migrations continuing and concentrating, but a new injection of species has arrived on the scene. Galapagos now.

Perhaps the dyslexic solicitations of spam are in fact the early attempts to speak by the emerging singularity: the artificial intelligence network. Will these immaterial creatures help us find our way? Will they lead us safely through the silicone steppes? Or will they leave us to languish online, without so much as a mirage to fall into, cracked lips puckered for a kiss that never comes?

SHOULDN'T ALL.

Shouldn't all moments have the right to be momentous?

I Was Strolling.

I was strolling in a park in Barcelona. The park itself was dry and sprawling, with more dust and gravel than grass, but enough of the latter to convince some of the locals to take a nap or read a book during siesta time. Every fifteen minutes or so, this park was punctuated by enormous monuments, completely out of scale with the people, like corpses of fascist elephants. Sitting in the shade of one of these marble behemoths, on green metal chairs, next to a small fountain, I noticed a very appealing couple. She was well-dressed, in a fashionably anachronistic way, and could have been anywhere between 18 and 35. He seemed somewhat older, but still in the prime of his life, exuding a quiet, albeit slightly resentful confidence. They were playing chess, and I tried to ascertain, from the concentration on their brows, whose turn it was to move next. But neither one did. Every now and again she would tug at an earlobe, while he would say a quick witticism that would raise barely a smile. Pigeons cooed around their feet, but thankfully did not mistake them for statues. It occurred to me they were lovers, or at least once had been. But now here they sat, literally in a stalemate. And yet the couple were clearly resistant to starting over, or abandoning the game. Indeed, a few days later, after torrential rains, I found them again, at the same table, with the sparse and melancholy chess-pieces in the same desultory positions. Their clothes had reversed chromatically, but they still seemed incapable of any decisive mood. The scene became so oppressive to me, that I nearly approached the table to cut in, as one does at a ball, in order to save a lady from her dance partner, or her own foolish enthusiasm. But my ignorance of Spanish forbade such a move. And so I simply sat with them from a distance, an unacknowledged witness to their mutual inertia.

THE FRENCH.

The French have been known to describe people, especially women, in terms of organic engineering. Both genders can be heard
praising or criticizing a woman's "architecture," meaning the way
her body has been designed and put together. Some of these fabricated forms seem hospitable, others hostile. That is to say, some,
like Sacre Coeur, are sentimental and nostalgic. Others, like the
Eiffel Tower are aloof yet available. While others still, such as the
Centre Pompidou, seem to wear their hearts—and perhaps other
organs—on their sleeve. Indeed, the cleavage is described in the
same language as "le balcon," or balcony. In English, we go so far as
to say someone has a nice *build*, but do not explicitly link it to the
art of dwelling.

But if our bodies are examples of architecture, then who is the
architect? Must we be restricted to God or Darwin? More to the
point, who is the client?

I ponder these questions in terms of she that shadows me. Does she
rent her body? Her being? Or does she own it outright? Moreover,
what will replace the emotional moats and libidinal drawbridges of
yesteryear?

If Goethe is Correct.

If Goethe is correct in postulating that "architecture is frozen music," does that mean music is liquid architecture?

OTHER MUSIC.

Other Music is a store located on East 4th Street, just around the corner from Lafayette, in Gotham City. Its name is a direct reference to Tower Records, which used to sit aggressively across the road, casting its shadow over the indie kids who disdained the Top 40 hits and supergroups of the 1970s. The staff and clientele at Other Music were always very proud of the fact that they had opted for an alternative to the mass-produced and mass-marketed sonic swill one could find amongst the gaudy stacks of Tower Records. However, the new digital economy soon began to cull companies that were old-fashioned enough to hock material wares, such as compact discs, taking down the dinosaurs first. Today, Other Music is perched precariously on the same site, conscious of its current existence as a non-sequitur.

How terribly traumatic, to be suddenly deprived of one's Big Other.

THERE IS A GIRL.

"There is a girl," says the editor. "But I want to know more about her."

"So do I," replies the author.

LET US TRY.

Let us try to give some details then.

She is rarely a local of whichever city she decides to employ as the backdrop to reveal herself. Then again, there are occasions in which she knows the terrain like the back of her hand.

This hand is pale, dark, cinnamon. Flawless. Cuticle-chewed. Gloved and unloved. Or vice versa.

She is shy, yet self-assured.

Fleet of foot, yet pensive as a statue.

She is a current. A pulse. A shared singularity. A glittering seam.

She is tall, diminutive, curvaceous, and slim.

Ahhhh, you think I am talking of Woman?

Please! I am not so Romantically uncouth.

Rather, it concerns the precise technique—the exacting flick of the wrist—with which one folds up the fan.

"My eyes can never grow weary of quickly passing over this peripheral multiplicity, these radiating emanations of womanly beauty. Every particular point has its little share and yet is complete in itself, happy, joyous, beautiful. . . . Each one has her own, and the one does not have what the other has. When I have seen and seen again, observed and observed again, the multiplicity of this world, when I have smiled, sighed, flattered, threatened, desired, tempted, laughed, cried, hoped, feared, won, lost; then I fold up the fan, then what is scattered gathers itself together into a unity, the parts into a whole. Then my soul rejoices, my heart pounds, passion is aroused. This one girl, the one and only in all the world, she must belong to me; she must be mine."

If I am a man without qualities, she is a woman with too many.

WHERE EXACTLY.

Where exactly is this Point A and Point B that everyone keeps talking about, and traveling between? This must be the world's busiest road. Moreover, Point B must be far more populated than Point A by now, since people rarely seem to make the return journey.

THE INITIAL OYSTER BAR CRAZE.

The initial oyster bar craze in New York began around 1830 and ended in 1870, when it was pronounced that pollution from ever-growing maritime traffic had put an end to the safe harvesting of local oyster beds. Illustrations and restaurant reviews provide us with time machines for those splendid houses of worship, dedicated to this most ugly and delicious comestible. No doubt there was a hierarchy of establishments, from the outdoor din of South Street, where gutter-snipes searched for dropped coins amongst patron's feet, to the more refined and removed atmospheres around Wall Street, where women would pause in the cold scrape of cutlery to suck at the soft inside of these spiky shells, their ostrich feathers pluming from their satin-lined hats, irritatingly bobbing hither and thither, tickling the noses of those at the next table.

A LITTLE FURTHER UPTOWN.

A little further uptown, there was the infamous Bowery in its original squalor, of which only crusty residues remain. (Ironic, of course, that "bowery" originally meant "country seat.") No oysters were served here, given the grim and unforgiving conditions of the slums. The only hope for many was a drink that began as a rumor, but evolved into a genuine last resort. Known as "the solution," it was served in a saloon of ill-repute on the corner of Houston Street. No matter how stout or strong of constitution, the man who downed a glass of this libation would never walk out of the place again. Indeed, would never have to worry about *anything* again.

NOWADAYS.

Nowadays there is no evidence of oyster bars by the waterfront, unless you count Long John Silver's takeout in the food court of Pier 17. And it is impossible to order "the solution" even from the roughest of drinking establishments, forcing people to commit suicide homeopathically. Glass by glass. Which begs the question, can we register our collective losses without succumbing to nostalgia?

Turning my gaze further out into the water, where the East River meets the Hudson, I hope to spy her: the pirate's daughter, riding astride a sea-turtle, all the way from south of the equator.

With a Population.

With a population of 21,500, Belgium's town of Gembloux, in the Southern province of Namur, is in no danger of being described as a city. Founded in the 10th century, this large hamlet features a Benedictine Abbey, an Agronomical College, a Renaissance Town Hall, and—situated near a "beguiling park"—a small cutlery museum. (To arrange a tour, call 081-626330.) One is inclined to wonder, however, what the tipping point might be between a large kitchen and a small cutlery museum. Twenty knives? Fifty spoons? Three rare dessert forks?

ALSO IN NO DANGER.

Also in no danger of being spoken in the same breath as the great cities of the world is the town of Cattaraugus (pop. 1075), in western New York state. One Patrick Cullen, president and CEO of the Bank of Cattaraugus, as well as unofficial town spokesman, has ruffled feathers in the cutlery world by suggesting that the new American Museum of Cutlery (716-257-9813) is "unique in the Western Hemisphere." Clearly this institution has access to an impressive variety of eating utensils, given that the town lives in the withered bosom of a region which once boasted one-hundred-and-fifty cutlery companies. (Only six now remain.) The museum features "the full spectrum of cutting tools." And yet there is no mention of Gembloux, which—if our traditional maps are to be believed—resides within the Western Hemisphere.

The plot thickens, however, when we consider Laguiole in France (pop. 1296), which also resides in this same cartographical quadrant, and which *also* claims to have an inimitable Cutlery Museum (05-6548-43-34).

No doubt letters have been exchanged. A pecking order has been established, then reversed. After lobbying comes espionage, and even sabotage. For the good Lord knoweth that there is room not in the Western Hemisphere for three cutlery museums. And so, knowing full well the murderous capacity of a vexed Belgian, or a furious Frenchman, we should urge Mr. Cullen to lie in bed with his back to the wall, lest he want to sleep forever with a fondue fork betwixt his shoulder blades.

CITIES ARE VORACIOUS.

Cities are voracious. They devour villages that stand in their way, absorbing them deep into clotted arterials. This famously happened to Greenwich Village, whose serendipitous, winding streets suggest a previous independence, before the grid imposed its uncompromising angles on the entire island. This also happened to Highgate and Hampstead, two idyllic villages which were once a day's horse ride from London, but now perch rather awkwardly on the tedious Northern Line.

Walking around Hampstead Heath, it is possible to recall this more pastoral time, when certain noble oaks dip their branches long and low, so as to form a perfect seat for a lady to sit comfortably side-saddle, while pressing petals into her favorite primer—all the while hoping each figure cantering over the horizon is her appointed *rendezvous*. Here among the bowers, it is difficult to believe in the "greater London," with its business parks, gated communities, and profligate prostitution to the new economy. "His love of people as they are stems from his hatred of what they might be."

The sun has long set on the British Empire. And yet there are summer evenings when the sun barely moves, indeed seems to travel, inch by inch, backwards in the sky. Here Alice snoozes by the village green, the white rabbit under her arm. And families dressed in their Sunday best linger over picnics with deceased aunts and uncles, in the warm crepuscular necropolis of Highgate Cemetery.

I Hear.

I hear she is now in London.

One source (who cannot entirely be trusted, it is true) claims that she was seen dining the previous week with a gentleman friend.

Was he, by chance, an architect, admiring her flawless décor?

In any case, my favorite city moves with her.

CUTLERY POEM.

As knife falls,
we fork,
and then spoon.

TINY HOLES IN THE FLOORBOARDS.

Tiny holes in the floorboards, along with a stuffed sparrow that had been killed by a lusty cover drive by W.G. Grace, are all I remember with any conviction from my personal tour of the Long Room at Lord's famous cricket ground. These holes had been made by a century and a half of batsmen (some amateur, some professional) striding in spiked shoes from the dressing rooms to the pitch, twirling their bats of finest willow, the spikes on the bottom of their shoes wholly inappropriate for such a formal setting. Jovial men with large moustaches would watch each batsman stroll to the crease, offering good luck or a good-natured ribbing, depending on the team. Intimidating men, also with large moustaches, would offer no words at all, since they were rendered in oil paint.

No doubt it was called "the Long Room" as much for its capacity to distort the passing of time, as much as its elongated architecture. The forty paces or so in full padding would seem so much longer during the journey back to the pavilion after being dismissed by the umpire. Walking disconsolately back through a gallery of disappointed gentlemen after failing to maintain one's wicket must have been a highly humiliating experience. Then again, these forty paces would seem all the sweeter during a triumphant inning: something known to the greats of the game, all of whom have passed through this *rite de passage*, leaving their anonymous marks as a gift to the gods of earnest contest.

Some believe, including my enthusiastic Cockney tour-guide, that an expert can spot the tracks left by different players, with the almost supernatural instincts of an Aboriginal tracker. These holes here, for instance, near the leather sofa, were made by Sir Garfield Sobers. These over here, by the whisky cabinet, were made by Sir Geoffrey Boycott. And these ones by that knot in the wood, were left by Sir Donald Bradman.

Even though I realize now that my tour-guide could not have possibly been able to discern one set of spikes from another, these holes left an impression on me, far deeper than the half-inch in the floorboards. Their very enduring indexicality seemed like miraculous proof that these names had been connected to real people, who tied laces, and sweated profusely and hit sixes.

Here in this idyllic village green, surrounded by a soupy sea of city grey.

BLISSFUL IS THE ROAD.

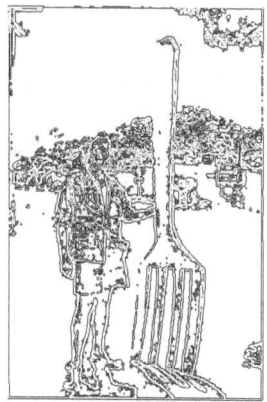

Blissful is the road which never forks, but merely winds. Blessed be the traveler on such a road, with no point of bisection: no need to make a decision of resolve or of navigation (two terms which amount to the same thing). When confronted with such a choice, the poet took the one less traveled by. Wiser, however, is the Zen sportsman, who said: "If you come to a fork in the road, take it."

To the Untraveled.

"To the untraveled, territory other than their own familiar health is invariably fascinating. Next to love, it is the one thing that solaces and delights. Things new are too important to be neglected, and mind, which is a mere reflection of sensory impressions, succumbs to the flood of objects. Thus lovers are forgotten, sorrows laid aside, death hidden from view. There is a world of accumulated feeling back of the trite dramatic expression: 'I am going away'."

WE ARE TOLD.

We are told that Kierkegaard was called "the Fork" as a child because of his uncanny ability to find people's weaknesses, and then stick his mental utensil into them. This historical tidbit crossed my mind soon after a young gypsy girl, surely no older than five, stabbed me repeatedly on the back of the hand with a dirty toothpick, as I sat outside a café in Rome, trying to enjoy a cup of coffee. She did this to demonstrate her displeasure with my unwillingness to give her money, even when asked nicely. Her tactic worked, as I sharply withdrew my hand, and gave her a couple of coins. She then smiled a sweet smile, revealing a single gold tooth. It occurred to me that her family, no doubt watching this transaction from the shadows, was using their daughter's mouth as a bank for their modest savings. And I shuddered to think what would happen when they decided to make a withdrawal.

SHE HAS RETURNED.

She has returned to my orbit.
She is present, but oblique.
Questions are answered politely, but on the diagonal.
She dresses to entice.
Fishnet stockings: a dragnet for the sons of Neptune.
(Or should that be Jason?)
Her legs, an academic lesson in "cool Medea."

THROUGHOUT THE CITY.

"Throughout *The City in History*, Lewis Mumford favors the cool or casually structured towns over the hot and intensely filled-in cities. The great period of Athens, he feels, was one during which most of the democratic habits of village life and participation still obtained. Then burst forth the full variety of human expression and exploration such as was later impossible in highly developed urban centers. For the highly developed situation is, by definition, low in opportunities of participation, and rigorous in its demands of specialist fragmentation from those who would control it. For example . . . in reading a detective story the reader participates as co-author simply because so much has been left out of the narrative. The open-mesh silk stocking is far more sensuous than the smooth nylon, just because the eye must act as hand in filling in and completing the image, exactly as in the mosaic of the TV image."

WHY IS IT?

Why is it good to unwind, but bad to unravel?

But I Do Wonder.

"But I do wonder whether all of today's youth, while spectacular, is wasted, like fireworks in the middle of the day." This pithy observation goes around my head as I stroll unenthusiastically through Camden Town, wondering why all these colorful species of subcultures, this greater assembly of fowls, have little or no impact on the environment or the ambience. Perhaps the City of London has, under the auspices of New Labor, developed a secret program to coat the streets with a fusion of Teflon and soot, which means nothing sticks, yet still looks grimy. Nothing matters, yet still looks spent.

Indeed, when in the forsaken British capital, one could be forgiven for thinking that footpaths are actually conveyer belts, moving people past the same scrolling background of a typical new economy High St. . . . Boots Pharmacy, WH Smith news agency, H&M clothing store, Starbucks coffee shop, Boots Pharmacy, WH Smith news agency, H&M clothing store, Starbucks coffee shop, *ad infinitum*. Like a looped cartoon backdrop, repeating the same subliminal street features to save on costs.

Margaret Thatcher ruled this city with an iron fist and steel hair, crushing all resistance without blinking. For his part, Tony Blair continued the apocalypse via a new spin: with positive energy and positronic rays, which leave everything standing as before, but somehow scrambled their molecular make-up, sucking the marrow out of objects and people alike. International commerce has been welcomed here with splayed legs and open buttocks, and the locals have found that the imperial backwash doesn't taste so good. "London, that great cesspool into which all the loungers and idlers of the Empire are irresistibly drained."

Cracks and reforms and bursts in the violet air
Falling towers

Jerusalem Athens Alexandria
Vienna London

THE FIRST DAY IN ROME.

The first day in Rome I see a priest asleep in his confession booth, a little red light glowing for any passing sinful souls. I see glass elevators squeezed between ancient sandstone buildings. I see a sun shower swirling through the roof of the Pantheon. I see tour groups winding through the streets like Chinese dragons that have shed their scales, and their ethnicity, but retained their serpentine determination. I see a recent refugee in the Campo de Fiori, trying to sell a megaphone by talking into it. "Hello megaphone. Hello megaphone."

The medium is the message.

A Constant Battle.

A constant battle is waged in Rome between the nobility and the nubility. Sun-kissed women, drunk on the sap of their own youth, health, and beauty, enjoy the possibility of usurping their more wealthy and established sexual adversaries through the architecture of their bodies.

Here the cobblestones remind them of time's merciless maw, chewing hungrily on stiletto heels.

Scooters buzz through the eternal streets, under a Kleinian blue twilight sky.

A priest, nearly knocked from his virtuous thoughts, crosses himself, and continues across the square.

Vespers at dusk.

On the Train to Positano.

On the train to Positano, I meet two caricatured septuagenarian Southern Belles from Macon, Georgia. One is talkative, the other almost silent. The first asks, "are you of Italian extraction?" To which I shake my head. She then launches into a monologue, several sentences of which begin with the phrase, "My present husband." Eventually she catches herself, with the hint of a blush and a flirtatious grin. "My present husband," she says, lampooning herself. "Doesn't that sound *awfully* temporary?"

Legend Has It.

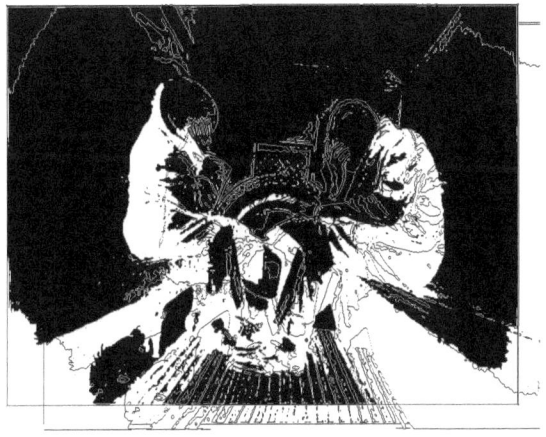

Legend has it that the Sirens sung ships to their doom from the dramatic cliffs around Positano. Indeed, the town itself is said to have been founded by Poseidon himself, as a gift to his favorite nymph, Pasitea.

The sirens in New York City—whether they be police, fire or ambulance—have the opposite goal of those situated near the Mediterranean. They seek to push people away, rather than lure them toward. (Unsuccessfully, sometimes, as in the case of sleazy lawyers, opportunistic photographers, and morbid gawkers.)

IN THE MID-19TH CENTURY.

In the mid-19th century, seventy five percent of Positano's eight thousand inhabitants took the same steam-ship destined for New York City. Instant depopulation!

Concerning this town, which clings to the cliff face in defiance of gravity, Paul Klee is said to have claimed: "It is the only place in the world conceived on a vertical rather than a horizontal axis." But what about New York?! Is that why the citizens of Positano fled to the capital of the New World? Did the oracle tell them that there would be higher dwellings? Higher than the sea-eagles? Higher than the clouds, even? With ghostly elevation machines, that sometimes stop of their own accord?

Who knows if these humble fisher-folk had an inkling of the future, and the techno-mythic city they would help to construct? For it is possible that they were simply trying to escape the infernal song of the Sirens, which claimed their sons and husbands, and deprived them of sleep.

WE TALK.

We talk of "emotional baggage," but not emotional *luggage*.

What would Koichi make of this?

CITIES GIVE US COLLISION.

"Cities give us collision." So wrote Ralph Waldo Emerson in 1860. Around this date the very word "collision" was in the process of changing its meaning from a decidedly non-violent and harmonious "coming into contact" with the more jolting definition we are used to today. The fact that this change was also contemporary with the first railway accident is no . . . well . . . *accident*. The poets and essayists have written stanza upon tome about the rude shock of urban life: wheels crushing feet, elbows nudging earlobes, horses kicking ganglia, and so on. And yet, according to the perfect symmetrical logic of cartoon amnesia, the second jolt may help us wake up to ourselves. "London and New York," continues Emerson, "take the nonsense out of a man."

THE GENDER OF A GIVEN CITY.

The gender of a given city has been the subject of much speculation. Paris, *par example*, is a man, according to John Berger, and a woman, according to Angela Carter. New York, according to the latter, is "a well-adjusted transsexual." How a city personifies itself is an intriguing phenomenon, leading to questions of not only gender but ethnicity, age, sexual orientation, politics, and all those other qualities and criteria used to match people on dating sites. In which case, Canberra is a grizzling boy scout with a scrape on his knee, Geneva a painted, withered harlot with a genuine smile, Amsterdam a shrewd businessman who dresses younger than he should, and Hong Kong a beautiful movie starlet that has recently escaped the clutches of her lecherous stepfather, only to marry an old tyrant.

THE GENIUS.

The genius (or tragedy, depending how you look at it) of hetero-sexuality boils down to this: the two lovers desire a different ob-ject. The man lusts after the woman. The woman after the man. Meaning, they cannot truly *share* that which is most important to them. Just as the seducer wants the seduced to share in his or her triumph, or the master seeks the complicitious recognition of the slave, we have an impossible structural situation. This keeps the libidinal economy between the genders in motion. But it also en-sures there is neither boom nor bust. Heterostatic equilibrium.

Were Lacan a Political Pundit.

Were Lacan a political pundit in the 1990s, he would have vindicated Bill Clinton's notorious statement during the latter's impeachment. He would have done so according to his own dictum that "there is no sexual relationship."

Ergo.

He did not.

Have sex.

With that woman.

Miss Lewinsky.

ANTONIO AND GIUSEPPE.

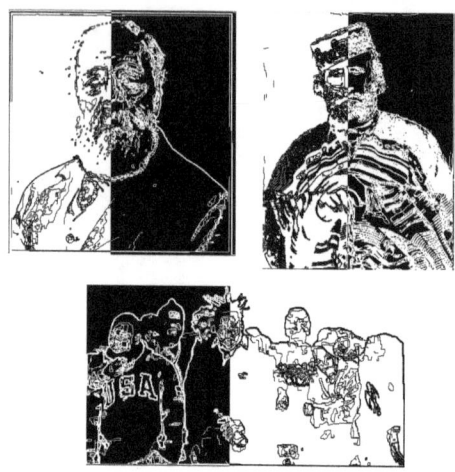

"Antonio and Giuseppe were like many other Italian immigrants who had fled Europe in 1848 after failed revolutions swept the continent. Upon meeting in America, the two took a small house on Tompkins Avenue in the Clifton section of Staten Island, where Antonio worked on his electrotherapy machines and Giuseppe made smokeless candles. But Antonio and Giuseppe weren't like the others. The former's surname was Meucci and the latter's was Garibaldi. One invented the telephone [many years before Alexander Graham Bell tried to claim that honor] and the other unified Italy."

More than a century-and-a-half later, the descendents of African Slaves, collected under the moniker of The Wu Tang Clan, used their own "electrotherapy machines" to make a new kind of popular talking music. In this music, they often refer to their home borough of Staten as "Shaolin."

FORBIDDEN CITY PACKAGE TOURS.

"Forbidden City package tours."

"One time forbidden, now time welcome."

"Act fast, and come in China."

"See performing Shaolin monks."

"Save more when book online."

Economists Talk.

Economists talk of "global value chains."

I find this a beautiful phrase.

But I suspect the values it evokes in me are very different to the ones they have in mind.

THE DUTCH HAVE A SAYING.

The Dutch have a saying: "Better homesick than Holland."

Every nation should have this attitude.

On the Other Hand.

On the other hand, there is a type of homesickness which comes from the inability to *escape* home. From *too much* home. (A being-sick-of-home, as Heidegger might have said, were he capable of such . . . were he allergic to blood and soil.) No doubt we are all carriers. Human spores. Infected vectors. And even if we reject many aspects of our culture, there is little we can do to avoid the super-saturation of its influence. That is to say, there is a very Australian way of being anti-Australian, a very Dutch way of being anti-Dutch . . . and so on.

The Call to Prayer.

The call to prayer echoes throughout the twilight city of Istanbul, each staggered from the other like theological car alarms. For the faithful, it is the signal to suspend earthly doings and to display punctual devotion. They are figures who have temporarily escaped an ornate medieval clock, shepherded back to their neighborhood Mosque, and animated by a mechanism that I am not trained to fathom. For my American expat hosts, however, this early evening cacophony is known simply as the "call to cocktails." And who am I to shun local custom?

THE CITY'S POET LAUREATE.

The city's poet laureate describes the invisible mist that clings to the walls, streets, and hearts of Istanbul as *Hüzün*: a collective form of melancholia exhaled from within the very particles of breath of the residents. These are orphans of empires, layered one upon the other like the rugs of the local merchants. *Hüzün* coats the slightly furry skin of obscenely ripe figs, just as it does the body-language of the young gathered in nightclubs, voting with their hips to straddle Asia and Europe (the former by day, and the latter by night). It is the flotsam of the new jet set—an oppressive awareness shouldered by the indigenous population, that greatness lies further behind each day, despite Ataturk's spectral and omnipresent promises. Perhaps this explains the thinly-veiled hostility shown to tourists, who follow in the footsteps of Byron in search of glimpses of Roman, Byzantine, or Ottoman pentimentos. I begin to wonder if I would have sensed this morbid belatedness at all, if I had not read about it first. That's the problem with poets. They can give an entire city a disease it did not have, through the mere act of diagnosis.

THEY CAN PRINT STATISTICS.

"They can print statistics and count the populations in hundreds of thousands, but to each man a city consists of no more than a few streets, a few houses, a few people. Remove those few and a city exists no longer except as a pain in the memory, like the pain of an amputated leg that is no longer there."

THERE IS A SURPRISING ABSENCE.

There is a surprising absence of steam in a real Turkish bath—at least in the venerable one I now find myself. Nevertheless, intense heat radiates off the glistening, ornate tiles, and beads on my skin: not pale enough to be outed immediately as European, but not dark enough to be mistaken for a Turk. The effect is of being naked in an ancient Church, while the sensation is giddy: a kind of pleasant, sensual vertigo. I lie face up on the stone slab at the center of the *hamam*, and gaze at the light spearing through the crescents carved into the dome. Yes, it is said Byron bathed here, and I cannot help but wonder if the ancestors of his own impassioned bacteria could be found here today, wedged between the crevices of the stone basins that extrude from the wall like petrified orchids. A chubby German-speaker, now mute with tension, is being pounded and pummeled by one of the surly attendants: yanked this way and that, soaped and rubbed with abrasive mitts until he looks sunburnt, and on the brink of tears. I half-watch, rather smug in my good sense not to get the "full treatment," as two men now treat this naked, brutalized visitor like a giant baby, flipping him over and spinning him around, as his eyes plead to the humid heavens for mercy. Were this happening in the street, I would call for the police. But here the soggy slapping sounds are simply part of the architecture.

THE WOMEN'S BATHS.

The Women's Baths, nestled above Coogee Beach in Sydney, are, as the name suggests, for women only. So as long as you have a vagina and a mere twenty cents, this allegedly bewitching oasis is open for your pleasure. I say "alleged" because I am not blessed with the first of these conditions for entry, and thus it exists solely in my imagination. Both my mother and sister enjoy ditching me and my stepfather at the gates, which reveal only a tree-lined path, winding down the cliff face. (What's the name of those trees? I don't know. I must find out.) They emerge several hours later, with tales of Arabic women, liberated from their burkhas, frolicking in feminine formations to the sound of belly-dancing music, blasting from a portable stereo. There are also graceful mermaids of all ages, and sleek Sapphic water-nymphs basking topless in the sun. Perhaps even *she* is waiting for me there, despite all layers of logic.

The whole scene suggests a mythical version of the Gynaeceum, a place reserved only for women and one lucky man, as described by every libidinal traveler from Marco Polo to Gustave Flaubert.

But then I realize my mother and sister make up some of the scene. And no doubt other people's mothers and sisters, with peeling shoulders and heat rashes, wearing lurid flip-flops and mismatched hats, and generally embodying the reality principle as vividly as they do unwittingly.

And so I realize it's best not to spend the twenty cents in order to save my own priceless fantasies.

EACH GUEST IS GIVEN ACCESS.

Each guest is given access to a private changing room, with a small bed and various Old World finishings and niceties. It smells of leather, tobacco, and lingering, anonymous masculinity. Were there a minor earthquake, one could be forgiven for believing oneself inside a sleeper on the Orient Express. But today the walls are still. My limbs buzz with a delicious fatigue, and my mind breathes in the most shameless, pre-fabricated Orientalist fantasies. She feeds me soft cubes of Turkish delight, washed down with mint tea. She smokes a fragrant cigarette, wrapped in purple paper, monogrammed with her own initials in gold. She coos to the white peacocks, as if intimate with their mute, watchful language. Her skin is the color of Iranian saffron. Guilty pleasure. A tautology.

But there is little chance of really encountering her here. The sexes are strictly segregated. Better luck, perhaps, in the Grand Bazaar, of which one local told me, without trying to offend (merely stating the obvious): "There are beautiful things there, but not for you." Here the labyrinth could spiral so far into the distance that one could conceivably emerge through the fairy chimneys of the subterranean cities of Cappadocia. Or, even further, inside the winding alleys of Chunking Mansions.

The cities have folded again. Ontological origami.

But upon shaking myself awake, against the voluptuous G-forces of both *hamam* and *hüzün*, I recall my true location.

I am in Istanbul, where every corner reveals a smattering of stray cats, in various states of plaintive disrepair.

I am in Istanbul, where the breakfasts are biblical: honey, olives, cheese, nuts, dried fruit.

I am in Istanbul, where male tourists flinch in surprise, as the barber deftly uses a match to burn the hair from inside their ears, like some kind of magic trick.

I ENCOUNTER.

I encounter a woman of indeterminate age, and she consents to dine with me. However, I can tell within moments that it is not her. Nevertheless, I am happy to have some Anglophone company, especially from a local, who can give me some sense of the daily choreography whirling around me. She explains the elaborate rules of romantic discourse in Persian cultures. For instance, a woman is expected to say "excuse me for turning my back" when obliged to do such a thing, while the man is expected to reply, "a flower has no back." She also notes that the concept of a crush is foreign to the Turkish heart, since men especially are expected to leap straight from fondness to overwhelming near-suicidal passion (which does not, of course, exclude regular infidelity on both sides).

I tell her my theory that Turkish Delights are designed to look like the powdery, glowing coals on top of the hookah water-pipe, fabricated by some brilliant medieval confectioner, who came up with this *trompe l'oeil* in a moment of smoky inspiration. She looks at me like a slow child, who has only now figured out that the sun rises in the East every morning.

I Would Like.

I would like to be one of those men you see in the old-school barber shops. Not getting a haircut. Not working there. Just sitting in a chair, reading the paper, and adding to the conversation now and again.

You know, those guys.

THE JAPANESE.

The Japanese are extremely punctilious. A bit like the Swiss, if the Swiss were distributed along the continuum of eccentric to crazy. Indeed, the Japanese dedication to duty and attention to detail—no matter how trivial or futile—inspires goose bumps of admiration. I notice a goth-lolita girl, stylized black top-hat barely bigger than a cupcake, perched at an angle on her head, playing a video game that boasts a ukulele as interface. Her face is a study in concentrated absorption. I see a man in uniform, holding an electric blue glow-stick, walking in patient circles around a road worker, repairing a pothole in the rain. I see a woman bowing slowly and regularly, like a Geisha automaton, to greet customers at a shopping mall. (I watch her for five minutes, and cannot be certain of her status as human or machine.)

Conversely, I read a story in the newspaper about a man from Shibuya who had killed himself the previous day, because the government had cancelled his social security benefits. It seems he had given up actively looking for work. The deceased left a simple suicide note: "I just want to eat a rice ball."

This City.

"This city can be known only by an activity of an ethnographic kind: you must orient yourself in it not by book, by address, but by walking, by sight, by habit, by experience; here every discovery is intense and fragile, it can be repeated or recovered only by memory of the trace it has left in you: to visit a place for the first time is thereby to begin to write it: the address not being written, it must establish its own writing."

AKIHABARA.

Akihabara (otherwise known as "electric town") is the part of town residents of Tokyo go to buy everything from digital music players to sex robots dressed as French maids. I find myself wandering rather aimlessly in a giant, multi-level electronics store. This is a family concern, however, so no sex robots are on display. Nevertheless, the escalator ushers me towards a surreal scene, on par—in terms of unexpected epiphany—with Wordsworth's field of daffodils. Only this is an artificial field, populated with robotic horses. The horse itself, however, is missing, leaving only a mechanical saddle of various shapes, sizes, and juddering speeds. Not one of these animated saddles is dormant or unstraddled. Indeed, there is a line for the privilege of testing one out. So very incongruous, amongst the DVD players and vacuum cleaners is a drove of blank-faced housewives, bouncing to the unsynchronized rhythms of their acephalic machines. The popularity of the product is itself suspicious, and I think back to a history book I once read, dedicated to all the types of "social camouflage" afforded the female orgasm. But none of these women seem conspicuously aroused. Rather, they appear as robotic as the machines they are riding. And yet, I have the distinct feeling that if someone—their husband, for instance, or an over-zealous sales assistant—attempted to usher any one of them off the gently bucking plug-in creature, there would be an impassioned and negative response. Perhaps a handbag to the bridge of the nose, or an umbrella tip to the sternum.

And so I leave them to it: this band of middle-aged Japanese women, home on the range. Dourly riding in one spot, yet into the fluorescent sunset.

IF HEIDEGGER.

If Heidegger is right in saying that, as humans, we are existentially "thrown" into the world as clay is thrown onto a pottery wheel, then it is no wonder that we feel rather glazed.

THESE DAYS.

These days, even devotees of Bataille aim for little more than "the practice of mild pleasure before death."

LET US CONSULT.

Let us consult the two-headed turtle.

To the left head, with a yellow stripe down to its nostrils, we say "absence makes the heart grow fonder."

To the right head, with red circles around the eyes, we say "out of sight, out of mind."

Tell us, two-headed turtle, which of these common truisms speaks the actual truth?

VIRTUALITY.

Virtuality is not the same thing as possibility, although it is intimately related to it. Structurally speaking, the virtual is to the actual as possibility is to reality, and yet the virtual evaporates in its own incarnation. In other words, once something *actually happens*, its potential energy has been sapped.

For instance, a banana peel, lying in the middle of the street, may or may not make somebody carrying a crate of eggs slip over in a slapstick collapse. Whether this happens or not is irrelevant to the amount of virtuality present within the object, and within the situation. Similarly, a hand, hovering over a secret beloved's knee, may or may not expose this secret by lowering the fingers on to flesh. A boy is a virtual man. A man is a virtual corpse. Friends are virtual lovers. Or enemies.

Some actualities are more inevitable than others, as each millisecond bifurcates and branches into parallel scenarios, only one series of which you will ever experience in real time. Potential energy is thus something like an intangible fan belt, or invisible rubber ring which loops around a generator, creating kinetic energy. Alternative moments sacrifice themselves in order to usher in the *being thus*.

Deep down we all know this. We understand that the world is powered by what *doesn't* happen.

ONE THING.

One thing is certain.
Reality does not occur in real time.

A CHILD PLAYS.

A child plays with a spool of thread.
His mother has left the room. Is out of sight.
From his raw understanding of things, existence has made an
  exception in her case.
Inconceivable.
Fort/da.
Here/there.
The child plays with the makeshift toy.
His game is born of agony.

To Intersect.

To intersect.

Over and over.

Again and again.

This is our new arrangement.

She assures me it is so. (And I choose to believe her.)

To pull cities together, and then push them apart. To feel their bricks crumble in our fingers like honeycomb, before fusing them once more between our palms. To hang the great capitals of the world from the crescent moon, like a nightwatchman's lamp. To fold them into origami birds that nest in our hats and pockets. To unpack them into radiant flotillas that span the placid oceans.

Together, we banish the pathos of the asymptote.

Apart, we disavow the tragedy of trajectories.

Geometry is our guild.

Divisible cities our province.

NOTES

—⚋—

MATTERING MAPS.

Lawrence Grossberg, *We Gotta Get Outta This Place: Popular Conservatism and Postmodern Culture.* New York: Routledge,1992.

Hakim Bey, *The Temporary Autonomous Zone, Ontological Anarchy, Poetic Terrorism.* New York: Autonomedia, 1985. [http://hermetic.com/bey/taz_cont.html]

J. G. Ballard, *Crash: A Novel.* New York: Picador, 1973.

Martin Heidegger, "The Age of the World Picture" (1938), in *Off the Beaten Track*, ed. and trans. Julian Young and Kenneth Haynes (Cambridge, Eng.: Cambridge University Press, 2002) vs. Gilles Deleuze, "What Children Say," in *Essays Critical and Clinical*, trans. Daniel W. Smith and Michael A. Greco. London: Verso, 1998.

MATERIAL GIRLS.

Theodore Dreiser, *Sister Carrie.* New York: Bantam Books, 1900.

SHE LOOKS DIFFERENT.

Gaston Bachelard, *The Poetics of Space* (1958), trans. Maria Jolas Boston: Beacon Press, 1969.

GILLES TREHIN.

Catherine Mouet & Gilles Trehin, *Urville*. [http://urville.com]

WHENEVER I HAPPEN TO BE.

E.M. Cioran, *History and Utopia* (1960), trans. Richard Howard. Chicago: University of Chicago Press, 1987.

IT'S SO HARD.

Cat Power, "Colors and the Kids," *Moon Pix*. Marador Records,1998.

THERE IS SOMETHING.

Laura Kipnis, "Adultery," *Critical Inquiry* 24.2 (1998): 289–327.

TELESYMBIOSIS.

J. Scott Turner, *The Extended Organism: The Physiology of Animal-Built Structures*. Cambridge, Mass.: Harvard University Press, 2000.

MARRIAGE.

The Invisible Committee, *The Coming Insurrection*. 2005. [http://libcom. org/library/coming-insurrection-invisible-committee]

DIVORCE OFTEN.

Friedrich Nietzsche, *The Genealogy of Morals* (1887), ed. Keith Ansell-Pearson, trans. Carol Diethe. Cambridge, Eng.: Cambridge University Press, 2007.

WALTER BURLEY GRIFFIN.

Letter from Charles Scrivener, New South Wales district surveyor. 1906. In Mark McKenna, *An Eye for Eternity*, p. 742. Melbourne: Melbourne University Publishing, 2011.
Jean Baudrillard, *America* (1986), trans. Chris Turner. London: Verso, 1988.

THE CAPTAIN COOK WATER FOUNTAIN.

Pierre Hubert, "Mon voyage à les Antipodes," unpublished diary. 1951.

IN THE RETRO-FUTURISTIC FILM.

F. Scott Fitzgerald, *Tender is the Night*. New York: Charles Scribner's Sons, 1934.

THE RHÔNE.

Joseph Conrad, *Under Western Eyes*. New York: Harper & Brothers, 1911.
John Lanchester, *The Debt to Pleasure: A Novel*. London: Picador, 1997.
F. Scott Fitzgerald, *Tender is the Night*. New York: Charles Scribner's Sons, 1934.
Jean-Jacques Rousseau, *The Confessions*. 1782.

I HAVE NO COUNTRY.

The Shanghai Gesture, trans. Joseph von Sternberg. United Artists, 1941.

WALKING.

Farid ud-Din Attar, *The Conference of the Birds.* 1177.
Geoffrey Chaucer, *Parlement of Foules* (c.1382), in *The Riverside Chaucer*, 3rd edn., gen. ed. Larry D. Benson. Boston: Houghton Mifflin, 1987.
Marshall McLuhan, *Understanding Media: The Extensions of Man.* London: Routledge and Kegan Paul, 1964.

THE ENTIRE BAR.

Frederic Jameson, "Postmodernism and Consumer Society," in *Postmodern Culture*, ed. Hal Foster. London: Pluto Press, 1985.
Ackbar Abbas, *Hong Kong: Culture and the Politics of Disappearance.* Minneapolis: University of Minnesota Press, 1997.

THERE IS AN ESSENTIAL DIFFERENCE.

Escape From New York, dir. John Carpenter. AVCO Embassy Pictures, 1981.

Giorgio Agamben, *State of Exception*, trans. Kevin Attell. Chicago: University of Chicago Press, 2005.

I SEEM TO BE.

Chungking Express, dir. Wong Kar-Wai. Miramax Films, 1994.

NEW YORK IS NOT REALLY.

McKenzie Wark, *Dispositions*. Cambridge, Eng.: Salt Publishing, 2002.

AN IMPOSSIBLE VOYAGE.

The engineer's name is "Mabouloff" in the original French transcription, meaning "Scatterbrain."

WE HAD TO.

Jean Baudrillard, *Fatal Strategies*. London: Semiotext(e): 1990.

I ATTEMPT TO CALCULATE.

Graham Harman, *Tool-Being: Heidegger and the Metaphysics of Objects*. Chicago: Open Court, 2002.

LIKE A CODEX.

Jean Baudrillard, *Fatal Strategies*. London: Semiotext(e), 1990.

NO CITY.

Roland Barthes, *The Empire of Signs*, trans. Richard Howard (1970). New York: Farrar, Straus and Giroux, 1982.
Italo Calvino, *Invisible Cities,* trans. William Weaver (1972). New York: Harcourt Brace, 1974.

THEY ARE PREPARED.

Rainer Maria Rilke, *The Notebooks of Malte Laurids Brigge: A Novel* (1910), trans. Stephen Mitchell. New York: Random House, 1982.

THE FRENCH.

Claire's Knee, dir. Eric Rohmer. Les Films du Losange, 1970.

IF GOETHE IS CORRECT.

Johann Wolfgang van Goethe, "Conversation with Eckermann, March 23, 1829." In *Conversations of Goethe with Johann Peter Eckermann*, ed. J.K. Moorhead, trans. John Oxenford. Cambridge, Mass.: De Capo Press, 1998.

LET US TRY.

Søren Kierkegaard, *Either/Or*. 1843.

ALSO IN NO DANGER.

Thomas Hartley, "Cattaraugus Opens New Cutlery Museum." Buffalo *Business First*, October 7, 2005: http://www.bizjournals.com/buffalo/stories/2005/10/03/daily44.html.

CITIES ARE VORACIOUS.

William Shakespeare, "Sonnet cxxvii." 1809. In *Shakespeare's Sonnets*, ed. William J. Rolfe. New York: American Book Company, 1905.
Theodor Adorno, *Minima Moralia: Reflections from a Damaged Life* (1951), trans. E.F.N. Jephcott. London: Verso, 2005.

BLISSFUL IS THE ROAD

Robert Frost, "The Road Not Taken," *Mountain Interval*. New York: Henry Holt, 1916.
Yogi Berra, *The Yogi Book: I Really Didn't Say Everything I Said*. New York: Workman Publishing, 1998.

TO THE UNTRAVELED.

Theodore Dreiser, *Sister Carrie* (1900). London: Penguin Classics, 1981.

THROUGHOUT THE CITY.

Marshall McLuhan, *Understanding Media: The Extensions of Man*. London: Routledge and Kegan Paul, 1964.

BUT I DO WONDER.

Douglas Coupland, *Shampoo Planet*. New York: Washington Square Press, 1992.

Shaun of the Dead, dir. Edgar White. Universal Pictures, 2004.

T.S. Eliot, *The Waste Land*. Horace Liveright, 1922.

Sir Arthur Conan Doyle, *A Study in Scarlet*.1886.

CITIES GIVE US COLLISION.

Ralph Waldo Emerson, "Culture," *The Conduct of Life*. 1876.

THE GENDER OF A GIVEN CITY.

John Berger, "Imagine Paris. A city, a Walk, a Metaphor," *Harper's Magazine*, January 1987.

Angela Carter, *Expletives Deleted: Selected Writings*. New York: Random House, 1992.

ANTONIO AND GIUSEPPE.

L Magazine, 2004.

FORBIDDEN CITY PACKAGE TOURS.

Babel Fish translation. [http://babelfish.altavista.com/]

THE CITY'S POET LAUREATE.

Orhan Pamuk, *Istanbul: Memories and the City*. New York: Vintage International, 2006.

THEY CAN PRINT STATISTICS.

Graham Greene, *Our Man in Havana: An Entertainment*. London: William Heinemann, 1958.

THE WOMEN'S BATHS.

Marco Polo, *The Travels of Marco Polo, the Venetian*. 1854 (revised Marsden translation).

Gustave Flaubert, *Flaubert in Egypt: A Sensibility on Tour*, ed. and trans. Francis Steegmuller. New York: Penguin Classics, 1996.

Busby Berkeley, "By a Waterfall." In *Footlight Parade*, dir. Lloyd Bacon. Warner Brothers, 1933.

THE JAPANESE.

Daily Yomiuri. 2007.

THIS CITY.

Roland Barthes, *The Empire of Signs*, trans. Richard Howard (1970). New York: Farrar, Straus and Giroux, 1982.

IF HEIDEGGER.

Martin Heidegger, *Being and Time*, trans. John Macquarrie and Edward Robinson. New York: Harper & Row, 1962.

THESE DAYS.

Georges Bataille, *Visions of Excess: Selected Writings, 1927-1939*, ed. and trans. Allan Stoekl. Minneapolis: University of Minnesota, 1985.

VIRTUALITY.

Gilles Deleuze, *Difference and Repetition* (1968), trans. Paul Patton. London: Athlone Press.

Sigmund Freud, *Beyond the Pleasure Principle* (1920), in *The Standard Edition of the Complete Psychological Works of Sigmund Freud*, Vol. 18, ed. and trans. James Strachey. London: Hogarth Press, 1978.

About the Author

Dominic Pettman is Professor of Culture and Media at Eugene Lang College, and of Liberal Studies at The New School for Social Research (formerly "The University in Exile"). He has also held teaching positions in Melbourne, Geneva, Amsterdam, and Paris. His books include *After the Orgy: Toward a Politics of Exhaustion* (SUNY, 2002), *Avoiding the Subject: Media, Culture and the Object* (AUP, 2004, co-authored with Justin Clemens), *Love and Other Technologies: Retrofitting Eros for the Information Age* (Fordham, 2006), *Human Error: Species-Being and Media Machines* (Minnesota, 2011), and *Look at the Bunny: Totem, Taboo, Technology* (Zero Books, 2013).

W. dreams, like Phaedrus, of an army of thinker-friends, thinker-lovers. He dreams of a thought-army, a thought-pack, which would storm the philosophical Houses of Parliament. He dreams of Tartars from the philosophical steppes, of thought-barbarians, thought-outsiders. What distances would shine in their eyes!

~Lars Iyer

www.babelworkinggroup.org